Fifty Fabulous Fables

Lida Brown McMurry

Contents

FIFTY FABULOUS FABLES

BY

Lida Brown McMurry

PREFACE

The fifty fables in this book have been selected for second grade reading because they are easily comprehended by pupils of that grade, and because they teach lessons which every child should learn.

It is not wise to tell the class the moral application of the fables. It is better to have each pupil make his own application without any suggestion from the teacher.

In adapting the stories the conversational form has been largely used; this form not only gives much pleasure to the children, but it also affords excellent opportunities for voice culture.

Most of the stories have been successfully used for several years with classes of children in the State Normal School at DeKalb.

FIFTY FAMOUS FABLES
THE TORTOISE AND THE DUCKS

"Take me with you, please," called a tortoise to a gray duck and a white duck that were flying over.

The ducks heard the tortoise and flew down toward him.

"Do you really wish to go with us?" asked the ducks as they came to the ground near the tortoise.

"I surely do," replied the tortoise. "Will you please take me?"

"Why, yes, I think we can do so," said the white duck slowly.

The two ducks talked together in low tones for a few minutes. Then they flew to the woods. They soon brought back a strong twig and dropped it in front of the tortoise.

"Now," said the ducks, "if we take you off to see the world, you must promise us one thing."

"What is that?" asked the tortoise. "I will promise almost anything if you will let me go."

"You must promise not to say one word while you are in the air, NOT ONE WORD," replied the ducks.

"All right, I promise," said the tortoise. "Sometimes I do not say a word for a whole day because there is no one to listen to me."

"Well, take firm hold of the middle of the twig; we are ready to start," said the gray duck.

"If you value your life, you must hold on tightly," said the white duck.

The tortoise took hold of the middle of the twig and each duck took hold of one end.

Then they flew up! up! up! while the tortoise swung from the middle of the twig. How he enjoyed it! He had never had such a ride.

They had gone a long way safely when they came to a hayfield. The haymakers looked up and saw the ducks and the tortoise.

"Ho! ho! the tortoise has stolen some wings," called one of the haymakers.

"What a queer carriage he has!" laughed another in a loud voice.

"I pity his horses," said another.

This made the tortoise so angry that he cried out, "You--" but no one knows what he was going to say, for he fell to the ground and was killed.[1]

THE MOUSE AND THE FROG

A frog, while out walking one day, saw a mouse coming toward him.

"There is that foolish mouse," said he. "I will play a good joke on him," and he grinned as he thought how much fun he would have.

---

[1] Adapted from The Tortoise and the Geese, in a book of the same name published by Houghton, Mifflin Co.

As they met, the frog said, "Good morning, Sir Mouse; I hope I find you well to-day."

"Very well," replied the mouse. "How are you?"

"My health is not very good, so I have taken a holiday. If you are not busy, what do you say to our spending the day together?"

"Good!" answered the mouse. "I have little to do and nothing would suit me better." So they started off together.

They had not gone far when the frog said, "Let me tie one of your front feet to one of my hind legs, so that I may not lose you."

"All right," replied the mouse. "We shall surely be fast friends then."

So the frog took a blade of grass and fastened one of the mouse's front feet to one of his hind legs. When the frog leaped, the mouse tumbled after. Then they stopped and had a big laugh; it was very funny.

They first went to an oat field, where the frog found many insects, and the mouse plenty of grain.

Beyond this field there was a pond. The frog had been going toward this pond all of the time, but the mouse had not noticed it. They were soon on its bank.

When the mouse saw the pond he cried out, "Oh, you know I do not like the water, Mr. Frog. Let us go to the barn."

"Nothing would do you so much good as a cool bath on this hot day. You have never taken one, so you can not know how good it will make you feel," and the frog jumped into the water.

The mouse tried to get free, but the frog only laughed.

A hawk, looking down, saw the mouse and swooped down upon it. Since the frog was fastened to the mouse, he too was carried off, and both lost their lives.

When the other frogs heard of what had happened, they said, "Served him right. Served him right," and no frog since that time has ever played a mean joke.

THE BOYS AND THE FROGS

"Let us go to the pond and have some fun," said George.

"What fun can we have there?" asked Frank. "The pond is nothing but an old mudhole. We can not swim in such water."

Down at the pond the sun shone warm, and an old mother frog and her children were sunning themselves on a log. Now and then one plunged into the water with a chug! and then crawled out on the bank.

That was a happy time in frog land.

In the midst of their play, they heard a sound which made the mother frog tremble. It was only a boy's laugh, but as soon as the mother heard it she said, "Into the water, every one of you. The giants are coming;" and they all jumped into the water.

The giants had armed themselves with pebbles. Each one had a pocketful. As soon as they caught sight of the frogs, they cried, "Now for some fun!"

Before the mother frog could reach the water, a stone hit her on one of her feet. The one-sided battle had begun.

Every time a little frog peeped out of the water to get a breath of air or to look at the two giants, whiz! flew a pebble right toward it, and it never cared to look at its enemies again.

The mother became very angry. She lifted her head boldly above the water.

"Cowards!" she cried. "If we could sting, would you fight us? If we could bite, would you be here? You have great sport tormenting us, because we cannot fight for ourselves. You are cowards! cowards!"

And all the little frogs echoed, "Cowards! cowards!"

THE SHEPHERD BOY AND THE WOLF

John was a shepherd boy. He cared for his father's sheep. As there were many wolves prowling about waiting for a chance to kill the sheep, John had to be very watchful.

Some men were harvesting wheat in a field not far from where the flock was feeding. One day they were startled by the cry, "A wolf! a wolf!" They looked up and saw John motioning wildly to them and pointing toward the sheep.

They threw down their sickles and ran to the flock. But they found the sheep quietly grazing, and there was no wolf to be seen.

"Where is the wolf?" they asked.

"I didn't say the wolf was here,' replied John, and he laughed loud and long as he saw the look of surprise in the men's faces.

"What do you mean, you young rascal, by fooling us so?" they cried.

If they could have caught John, they would have given him a sound whipping, but he had run out of their reach.

Not many days after, these same men heard the cry, "Wolf! wolf!"

"John is trying to fool us again," they said, and went on with their work.

John called again and again, and seemed in so much trouble that the kind-hearted men left their work and hurried toward the sheep pasture.

When they came to the pasture, they knew that John had been playing another trick on them. They looked for him, but could not find him. He had hidden in some bushes where he could look on and enjoy their surprise and anger. At last they went back to their work.

One day wolves did come. John was very much frightened. He ran to the men for help. They only laughed at him. "Oh, you have fooled us twice," they said. "You shall not have another chance."

"But the wolves are surely there," cried John. "They are killing the sheep. Do come and help!" The men kept on with their work and did not even look at John.

Before he could find anyone who would believe him, many of the sheep had been killed.

THE TWO GOATS

A small stream ran between two hills. Over this stream there was a very narrow bridge. If two persons came to the opposite ends of this bridge at the same time, one must wait for the other to cross before he could go over.

One morning, two goats, a black one and a white one, reached the opposite ends of the bridge at the same moment.

The black goat called out to the white one, "Hold on a minute; I am coming over."

The white goat replied, "No, I will go over first; I am in a hurry."

"No," said the black goat, "I will not wait for you. I am the older."

"You shall wait for me," roared the white goat as he stepped upon the bridge and started across.

"We'll see if I am to wait for you," said the black goat, and he too started across.

They met in the middle of the bridge.

"Go back and let me cross,' said the white goat, stamping his foot.

"Go back, yourself," replied the black goat, and he pushed against the other.

They were very angry. Each drew back. Their heads came together with terrible force. They locked horns. The white goat lost his footing and fell, pulling the black goat over with him, and both were drowned.

THE STRIKE OF THE MILL FEEDERS

The mill feeders of a great mill--the stomach--met together to talk over their trials.

The hands said, "We are tired of carrying grist to the door of the greedy mill. We would rather spend all our time painting pictures or writing books."

"We were made for talking and singing," said the lips, "but much of our time has to be spent in taking grist for the mill."

"And we," said the teeth, "give our life to crushing the grist which is brought to the mill. We are wearing out in its service, but what thanks do we get?"

"I have never had a holiday," said the tongue. "I do not mind talking, but I do not like to work for the mill. Three times a day or oftener, I must help the teeth to prepare the grist. I am tired of it."

The gullet said, "My whole life is given up to carrying the grist to the mill. I do not like such work. Let the mill feed itself. It has no business to work us to death."

"Let us all stop work," cried the mill feeders. "We will stop at once;" and so the mill shut down.

Many hours after, the lips said, "How strange that we should not feel like talking now that we have nothing else to do!"

The hands said, "We are too weak to paint or to write. We never felt so tired before."

The tongue became parched and all the mill feeders were unhappy.

More hours passed; then the mill feeders held another meeting. It was a short, quiet, earnest meeting.

"We have been fools," they all said. "The mill was working for us while we were working for it. Our strength came from the grist which we sent to it. We can do nothing without the help of the mill. Let us go to work again. If the mill will only grind for us, we will gladly furnish the grist."

THE FARMER AND HIS SONS

"Boys, why are you always quarreling? That is no way to live," said a farmer to his sons one day.

The sons would not listen to their father. Each wanted the best of everything. Each thought the father did more for the others than for him.

The father bore the quarreling as long as he could. One day he called his seven sons to him. He had in his hand a bundle of seven sticks.

"I wish to see which one of you can break this bundle of sticks," he said.

The oldest one tried first. He was the strongest, but he could not break it though he used all his strength. Then each of his brothers tried hard to break the bundle. None of them could break it.

At last they gave the bundle of sticks back to their father, saying, "We cannot break it."

The father untied the bundle and gave each son one stick.

"Now see if you can break the sticks," said their father.

They all said, "That is very easily done," and they held up the broken sticks.

"Now tell us why you asked us to break these sticks," said the sons.

"Do you not see," replied the father, "that if you all stand together, nothing can harm you; but if each of you stands by himself, you may easily be ruined?"

THE FOUR OXEN AND THE LION

"Those oxen are too good friends to suit me," said a hungry lion. "They are never far apart, and when I am near them they turn their tails to one another and show long sharp horns on every side. They even walk down to the river together when they become thirsty. If I could catch one of them by himself, I should have a feast."

But one day the oxen had a quarrel.

"The grass is freshest over in the valley," said one of them. "Let us go there."

"Oh, I don't like the grass there," said another. "It is better on the side of the hill. Let us spend the day there."

"I do not want to climb the hill," said the third ox. "The grass right here suits me best."

"I do not like any of the places of which you speak," said the fourth ox. "Come with me and I will find you the best grass you ever tasted."

"I am going to the valley," said the first ox. "You three may go where you please."

"And I shall go to the hill," said the second ox. "I think you are mean not to go with me."

"And I," said the third ox, "shall stay right here. You may all be sorry if you leave me. The lion may catch you."

"I am not afraid of the lion," said the fourth ox; "and if none of you will go with me, I shall go by myself to hunt a better pasture than any of you can find. I am older than you and I know where the best grass grows. You had better follow me."

"We will not do it," said the other three oxen. "You are not our leader if you are older."

So the four oxen separated. One went to the valley. The lion was down by the river and saw him coming. He waited quietly until the ox was very near; then he pounced upon him and killed him.

Then the lion looked about for the other oxen. One of them was feeding on the hill. He saw the lion coining, but, he could not get away. He could not defend himself with only one pair of horns; so he too was killed.

As the other two oxen were far apart, it was an easy matter for the lion to kill them also. And that is the way the quarrel ended.

THE HUNTER AND THE FARMER

"Are you afraid of a lion? I am not. There is nothing that I should like better than to meet one," said a man to his neighbor whose calf the lion had killed. "To-morrow morning I will go out and hunt for this fierce lion, which is doing so much harm. If he is anywhere about, I shall find him and kill him, and thus rid the village of fear."

The next morning the man started out alone to hunt the lion. He had, a gun and a sword. He looked so brave as he started off that the people in the village said, "What a blessing it is to have so fearless a man in our village! He will keep us from harm."

He walked several miles. At last he came near a jungle. He thought that the lion might have his home there. He asked a farmer whom he met if he had seen the tracks of a lion.

"Yes," said the farmer, "and I will show you where you can find him."

When the man heard this, he turned pale and trembled with fright.

"I do not care to see the lion," he cried. "I only wanted to see his tracks."

The farmer turned away in disgust, saying, "It is easy to be brave when you are out of danger."

THE FOX IN THE WELL

Once upon a time a fox fell into a well. He was not hurt by his fall. As there was little water in the well, he was in no danger of drowning; but he could not get out.

He cried, "Help! help! help! help!" but no one heard him.

By and by a wolf passed by the well. He heard the call. He looked into the well and asked, "Who is down there?"

"It is I," cried the fox. "I am glad that you have come to help me out."

"How did you get down there?" asked the wolf. "Have you been there long? Is the water very deep? Poor fellow, I do pity you! That is no place for you. You have a very bad cold, I see. I wish you were out."

"Please don't talk to me," cried the fox. "It is help I need. Do get me out and then I shall know that you are sorry for me."

THE MICE IN COUNCIL

What a queer meeting that was down in the cellar! There were big mice, little mice, old mice, young mice, gray mice, and brown mice, all very sober and thoughtful.

At last an old mouse spoke up and said, "Shall we have Mr. Graypate for our chairman? All those who wish Mr. Graypate to be chairman will please hold up their right hands." Every mouse raised a tiny paw.

Mr. Graypate walked out to the front and took charge of the meeting. It was well that they chose him, for he was the wisest mouse in the whole country. Gazing over the crowd, he said, "Will Mr. Longtail tell us why we have met here? Mr. Longtail, come out in front where we can hear you."

Mr. Longtail walked slowly to the front. Then he stood upon his hind legs and said:

"My friends, I think you all know why we are here. Last night Mrs. Whitenose, whom we all love, and all her family were killed by the big white cat. The night before, while Mrs. Blackfoot was out hunting, all her cunning little babies were killed by the same cat. Early this week one of my finest boys was killed. You or I may be next.

"Must we bear this and do nothing at all to save our loved ones and ourselves? We have met here to make some plan for our defense."

Having spoken, Mr. Longtail walked back into the crowd.

Mr. Graypate arose and said:

"You have heard why we are here. Anyone who has a good plan for ridding us of the cat will please tell of it. The meeting is open to all."

"Let us all run at him suddenly when he is not looking for us, and each give him a bite. That would surely kill him," said one brave mouse.

"But how many of us do you think he would kill?" said another mouse. "I will not risk my life nor that of my family." "Nor I"; "nor I"; "nor I," said many other mice.

"Let us steal his food and starve him to death," suggested another.

"That will only make him hungrier for mice," they replied. "That will never do."

"I wish we might drown him," said another; "but I don't know how we could get him into the water."

At last a little gray mouse with a squeaky voice went up to the front and spoke:

"I have a plan that will surely work. If we could know when the cat is coming, we could get out of his way. He steals in upon us so quietly, that we can not escape. Let us find a little bell and a string. Let us put the bell on the string and tie the string around the cat's neck. As soon as we hear the bell, we can run and get out of the cat's way."

"A very good plan," said Mr. Longtail. "We will ask our leader to say which mouse shall put the bell on the cat's neck."

At this there was a great outcry. One said, "I am so little that I can not reach high enough to bell the cat." Another said, "I have been very sick and am too weak to lift the bell"; and so the excuses came pouring in.

At last Mr. Graypate called to the crowd, "Silence! I shall choose no one. Who will offer to bell the cat?"

It was very quiet in the meeting. One after another of the younger mice went out. None but the older ones were left. At last they too went sadly home. No one would bell the cat.

THE FOX AND THE CROW

One day the door of a cottage stood open. A tame crow flew through the door into the cottage. She stole a piece of meat from the table, and flew to a branch of a tall tree.

Just as she had settled there to enjoy her meat a fox came along and stopped under the tree. He sniffed something good to eat. Looking about, he saw the meat in the crow's mouth and wanted it.

How could he get the meat? He could not climb the tree. What good would it do if he could? The crow would fly away when she saw him coming. He could not coax the crow to come down to the ground. She knew what a fox likes to eat.

At last the fox had a happy thought. He said to himself, "A crow is one of the proudest birds I ever knew. I will flatter her and she will forget about the meat."

So he called out in his sweetest voice, "Good day, my pretty bird"; but the crow did not reply. She only stepped about proudly on the branch.

"I wish I had such a beautiful form as you have," said the fox.

Still no answer, but the crow held up her head and turned it first to one side and then to the other, showing that she was pleased.

"What a graceful neck and bright eye!" said the fox. "The other birds may well be jealous of you."

No answer yet. She only raised her wings a little and gazed down upon the fox.

"If your voice were only as beautiful as your form and your dress, you would be queen of all the birds; but it seems that you can not talk at all. What a pity that you are dumb!"

The crow gave a loud "caw!" As she did so, the meat fell from her mouth. The fox snapped it up quickly.

Poor crow, she saw when too late that the fox was only fooling her.

THE VAIN CROW

"I hate a black dress, no matter how glossy," said a proud crow. "I have made up my mind to be a peacock."

As he said this, he flew away to a barnyard where he found some feathers which the peacock had shed. He picked these up with his bill and placed them among his own feathers.

Then he marched back and forth, looking at his fine new coat. He even tried to walk like the peacock.

The peafowls came into the yard. They did not know at first what to make of the sight. Then they saw that the crow was trying to dress and act as they did. They flew at him, calling, "Away with the cheat! Away with the cheat!" They pulled out all the peacock feathers and many of his own glossy black ones.

He was glad to get away alive, and flew back to his own family and old friends. But one of the crows had seen him in the barnyard and told the others how silly he had been acting.

"Where have you been?" they cried. "We know. We know. We will not have you in this flock. Away! away!" And they drove him from them.

Even the owls, whom he had always hated, made eyes at him and screamed, "Ch-ea-t! ch-ea-t!"

He flew into the forest. Here in a tree by a pond he lived a lonely life.

The tree-toads learned their queer song from him. This is his warning to them. "Don't, don't-be-cheat! Don't, don't-be-cheat!"

THE HORSE AND THE LOADED DONKEY

A man once owned a beautiful black horse and a very ugly donkey.

The horse always had plenty to eat and was well groomed, but the donkey was very poorly cared for.

One bright morning both animals were made ready for a long journey. A saddle was placed upon the horse, and a heavy pack of goods was loaded upon the donkey.

The donkey was a very patient animal. When well, he never complained of his hard lot, but this morning he staggered under the weight of his load. After going a short distance, he looked up at the proud horse and asked:

"Would you mind helping me to-day? I feel too ill to carry this heavy load. If you will help me, I shall soon be well and able to carry the whole load. If you refuse to help me, I shall surely fall by the way; then you will have to bear the burden alone."

The horse held his head very high while the donkey was talking; then he replied:

"Go on, you lazy beast! I am not a burden bearer. No, I will not take one ounce of your load."

The donkey groaned and moved forward a few steps, then fell to the ground dead.

The load was taken from the dead donkey's back and placed upon the horse.

At the close of the day the horse reached the end of his journey. Every bone in his body was aching, and he was so lame that he could hardly walk.

THE LEAVES AND THE ROOTS

"We cast cool shade upon the green grass," whispered the fluttering leaves. "We dress the tree in fresh and quiet green. It is bare and brown without us. The tired traveler and the panting beast are thankful for our shade. Children love to play under our shelter. At night the song birds of the woods fly to us for our protection. We hide the nests of mother birds. The light winds stay with us and caress us." And the leaves felt very proud and important.

"What you say is all very true, but you should not forget us," said a voice from the earth. "We are surely worth something."

"And who are you? Where do you grow?" asked the leaves.

"We are buried deep in the ground, far below you, but we feed the stem and make you grow. We are the roots. You owe your beauty to us. We are not beautiful as you are, but we do not die. Winter does not change us, but when it comes you fall. The tree stands firm, for it is held in place by us. If we should die, the tree would die and you would die with it."

THE BULL AND THE GNAT

A gnat perched upon the horn of a bull. "Dear sir," he said to the bull, "I am sorry to trouble you, but I am too worn out to go any farther. Does my weight tire you? When you can bear it no longer, I shall go on."

"You need not leave on my account," said the bull. "I did not know when you sat down and I shall not miss you when you leave."

THE FARMER AND HIS THREE SONS

A farmer who had worked hard all his life was taken sick. He knew that he must soon die. He called his three sons about his bed to give them some advice.

"My sons," said he, "keep all of the land which I leave you. Do not sell any of it, for there is a treasure in the soil. I shall not tell you where to hunt for it, but if you try hard to find it, and do not give up, you will surely succeed.

"As soon as the harvest is over, begin your search with plow, and spade, and rake. Turn every foot of earth, then turn it again and again. The treasure is there."

After the father died, the sons gathered in the harvest. As soon as the grain had been cared for, they planned to search for the hidden treasure. The farm was divided into three equal parts. Each son agreed to dig carefully his part.

Every foot of soil was turned by the plow or by the spade. It was next harrowed and raked, but no treasure was found. That seemed very strange.

"Father was an honest man and a wise man," said the youngest son. "He would never have told us to hunt for the treasure if it were not here. Do you not remember that he said, 'Turn the soil again and again'? He surely thought the treasure worth hunting for."

"Our land is in such good condition now that we might as well sow winter wheat," said the oldest son. His brothers agreed to this and the wheat was sown.

The next harvest was so great that it surprised them. No neighbor's field bore so many bushels of wheat to the acre. The sons were pleased with their success.

After the wheat was harvested, they met to make plans for searching again for the hidden treasure. The second son said:

"I have been thinking ever since our big harvest that perhaps father knew how this search would turn out. We have much gold, We did not find it in a hole in the ground, but we found it by digging. If we had not cultivated our fields well, we should not have had such a crop of wheat. Our father was wise; we have dug for the treasure and have found it.

"We will cultivate the ground still better next year and make the soil rich; then we shall find more treasure."

The other sons agreed to this. "It is good to work for what we get," they said.

Year after year the farm was well tilled and bore good crops. The sons became rich, and they had two things much better than wealth--good health and happiness.

THE YOUNG FOX

"You may hunt with me now, Reynard," said a wise old fox to his young son. "It is time that you were beginning to make your living."

"That pleases me well," said Reynard. "I should not mind going out alone."

"You are not ready yet to go by yourself. There are many things that I must teach you first. Do not go without me."

Reynard said nothing, but the next day, when his father was asleep, he went out into the field and brought home a nice, fat partridge.

He wakened his father by a quick bark and said, "See what I have caught. I do not need to go with you."

"You do not know what you need," replied his father. "No wise fox hunts in the daytime."

But Reynard did not mind what his father said, and every day he went out hunting. He killed so many chickens, turkeys and ducks that everyone tried to catch him.

One night the old fox started out alone, but Reynard crept slowly after him. The old fox went toward a large farmhouse. He stopped suddenly in the path and waited; then he ran on quickly.

Reynard followed. He stopped at the same place where the old fox had stopped.

"What is this?" he said. "A fine white turkey down in the grass! Well, well, is my father losing his sharp sight and his keen scent? I shall not let such a prize get away from me!"

He sprang upon the turkey. The trap gave a loud snap, and Reynard was a prisoner.

"What a fool I am!" he said. "I saw the bait. My father saw the trap."

VISIT OF THE MOUSE TO THE COUNTRY

"Mother, may I go into the country to-day? You said I might go some day. I am big enough now to go out alone. Do let me go," said Frisky, a young mouse, to his mother.

"Well, child, I can not be with you always. I suppose there must be a first time for you to go out alone. I dread to have you go, but if you will promise to run home if a cat comes near you, I will let you go," said Mrs. Gray, the mother.

"I will run, mother, if I see a cat. You know how fast I can go. I should like to see any cat catch me. I shall not be gone long. Good-by, mother," and off went Frisky.

Mrs. Gray watched him until he was out of sight. "I wish I had gone with him," she said. "He does not know the world as I do. I fear some harm will come to him," and she looked very much worried as she turned to go into her house. She tried to sleep, for she was very tired; but when she dozed she dreamed, and her dreams were all bad ones.

At last she went back to the door and looked for Frisky. He was coming, leaping along in a great hurry. He began talking to his mother before he reached her.

"Oh, mother," he said, "I met two big creatures on the other side of the pasture.

"One of them was very fine looking. She had very gentle ways. She stepped about so quietly that one could scarcely hear her. Her dress was of soft gray fur, much like yours, mother, and she wore whiskers like yours. I knew you would like to see her, so I was just going to invite her home with me when a terrible-looking creature came right toward me.

"He walked as if he were too good to step on the ground. His legs were naked, his toes were long, and his toe nails were strong and sharp. His dress was not so soft as yours. It was black and white. His mouth looked like a trap. I tell you, mother,

I should hate to get caught in that trap. On top of his head was something that wobbled as he walked. He straightened himself up, raised his arms and screamed. Such a scream! It nearly frightened me to death. He isn't coming, is he, mother? Do let me run into the house."

"My son," said his mother, stopping Frisky as he tried to pass her, "I shall not let you go out alone again until you know more.

"That animal which you liked so well and wished to invite to our house is a cat. It is the very one no doubt that killed all of your brothers and sisters when they were quite small. She would have killed you too at the same time if a dog had not come along and frightened her away. If you had gone close to her this afternoon, I should never have seen you again. I thought you would know a cat.

"The creature of which you were afraid cares nothing for us. He would not have harmed you. He has bare legs so he can wade about in the grass and not get his clothing wet. He uses those long toes and sharp claws to scratch in the earth for food. He does not catch mice with them. He uses that strong bill for picking up grain. People call him a rooster."

THE TWO DOVES

Two doves, White-coat and Blue-feather, lived in a dovecote. They were brothers and were very fond of each other. White-coat was a great home body, but Blue-feather liked to travel.

One day Blue-feather said to White-coat, "I want to see the world. This place is very tame. I have lived here all my life (he was only six months old) and have seen all there is to see. I want to visit other countries."

"Don't go, Blue-feather," said White-coat. "We have all we want to eat here, everyone is kind, and we have a good home. I have heard that in other places men set traps for birds or shoot them, and that sometimes large hawks swoop down and carry them off. You might be caught out in a storm and find no shelter; besides, it would almost kill me to be separated from you long. You might be able to bear it, but not I. Surely it is best to stay at home."

Just then a crow cawed. "Do you hear that crow, brother?" asked White-coat.

"It seems to say, 'You will be sorry if you go.' Do not go. Take his warning. See, too, it is raining. If you must go, do put it off until a better time."

"White-coat, why do you make such a fuss about nothing? I shall not be gone more than three days; then you shall hear of all the wonderful things I saw. I shall tell what happened to me from the beginning of my journey until its close. It will be almost as good as going yourself."

"I do not care about the world," said White-coat. "How can I let you go! You will find me watching for you at whatever time of day or night you reach home. I can not eat, I can not sleep, with you away."

At this, they said a sad good-by to each other, and Blue-feather flew away.

A dark cloud covered the sky. Blue-feather looked about for shelter. He flew to the only tree near, but its leaves could not keep off the driving rain, so his coat was wet through and through.

When the sky was clear again, Blue-feather left the tree and dried his plumage as he flew.

On the borders of a wood he spied some scattered grains of wheat. He was hungry and saw no reason why he should not pick them up. As he flew down, a snare was drawn about him. The wheat had been put there to tempt pigeons so that they might get caught. It was well for Blue-feather that the snare had been in use a long time and was rotten. By using his beak and wings he got loose, but he lost a few feathers out of his pretty coat.

A hawk saw him as he rose. Blue-feather was dragging a piece of the string which he could not loosen from his leg. The hawk was about to seize him. It seemed as if there was no help for him. But just at that moment an eagle caught the hawk and carried him off.

Blue-feather flew as fast as he could to a high fence, where he stopped to rest. He thought his dangers were over. He was very homesick.

While Blue-feather was sitting on the fence, a boy saw him. He nearly killed the poor bird with a shot from his sling.

Blue-feather was just able to fly. His leg was lame, and one wing was hurt, but he steered straight for home.

Late at night he arrived at his own dovecote, tired and hungry, but happy to be safe at home again. He found White-coat waiting for him.

White-coat smoothed his poor brother's feathers, nestled close to him, and soothed him with his coo! coo! coo!

THE HORSE AND THE WOLF

A horse, in the early spring, was turned into a pasture of fresh grass. He was enjoying himself very much when a hungry wolf spied him. The horse did not see the wolf.

The wolf said, "I want that horse. I have not had a good meal for a month. He is so big that I can not catch him as I would a sheep. I shall have to play a trick." So he lay down on the ground and thought how he could deceive the horse and then catch him.

"I have it," he said at last. "I will be a doctor. The horse is sound and well, but I will make him think that he needs a doctor; then I shall tell him that I can cure him." The wolf smacked his lips as he thought of the meal he would soon have.

He marched into the pasture in a very business-like way. Going right up to the horse, he said:

"Good morning, my dear sir. This is fine grass you are eating and a beautiful morning to be out. I am sorry to see you looking so poorly this bright day. I happen to be a doctor. As you know, a good doctor can tell at sight when one is sick. If you were well, you would not have been turned out to pasture. You know that there is much work to be done at this time of the year. Your master must think that you are not able to work.

"Now, my friend, be frank with me; tell me what ails you, that I may cure you. I have been to the best schools in the country. There I learned about diseases of every kind and a sure cure for every disease. If you have no money to pay my bill, do not let that trouble you. We can settle that later."

The horse looked at the wolf out of the corner of his eye and said, "Now that I think of it, I believe that something is wrong with the bottom of my left hind foot."

All the time the wolf had been looking for a good chance to spring upon the horse, but the horse did not let him get out of his sight for an instant.

When the horse told of his trouble the wolf replied, "Yes, I understand just what is the matter. There are many others having that same trouble this year. I have had as many as twenty cases. All are doing well. Let me look at your foot. Raise it now, please, care--"

At this instant the horse raised his foot, and with it gave the wolf such a terrible kick in his face that he fell heavily to the ground. The horse went on feeding.

As soon as the wolf was able to get up, he went groaning out of the field. He was cured of one thing, but the medicine was very bitter.

THE BIRDS, THE BEASTS, AND THE BAT

There was once a terrible war between the birds and the beasts. For a long time it was doubtful which would win.

The bat said, "I am not a bird and I am not a beast, so I shall fight on neither side."

At last the beasts seemed to be gaining the victory. The bat flew to them and said, "I am a beast. Look at my body and you will see that I am. I shall fight on your side."

New flocks of birds came to help their relatives, and the battle soon turned against the beasts.

Then the bat skulked over to the other side. "I am a bird," said he. "I can prove it by my wings," and he fought with the birds.

At last the war was over. The bat was hated by beasts and birds. Both made war upon him. He was obliged to slink off and hide in dark places during the day, never showing his face until dusk.

THE BEES, THE DRONES, AND THE WASP

Some working bees had made their comb in the hollow trunk of an oak.
The drones said, "We made that comb. It belongs to us."
"You did not make that comb," replied the workers. "You know very well that

you did not. We made it."

The drones answered, "That comb belongs to us and we are going to have it."

So the workers took the case to Judge Wasp that he might decide the matter.

The workers and the drones settled down before him. "You workers and drones," said he, "are so much alike in shape and color that it is hard to tell which has been seen in the tree. But I think the matter can be justly decided. Each party may go to a hive in which there is no honey, and build up a new comb. The one that makes comb and honey like that found in the tree is the owner of the tree comb."

"All right," said the workers, "we will do it;" but the drones said, "We will have nothing to do with such a plan."

So Judge Wasp said, "It is plain to see which of you made the comb. It belongs to the workers."

The drones buzzed away very angry, but they were not able to harm the workers or the judge, and the workers went back to their tree.

THE WOODMAN AND HIS AX

One day a poor woodman lost his ax. He hunted all day, but he could not find it. He was very sad, for how could he make a living for his family without an ax? Besides he had no money with which to buy a new one. As night came on, he sank down by the roadside and buried his face in his hands.

He heard a noise in the bushes and raised his head. A stranger was standing by him. "What is the matter?" asked the stranger. The woodman told him of his trouble.

"I am sorry your ax is lost," said the stranger. "Would you know it if you were to see it? I found an ax in the road. It may be yours. Is this it?" he asked, holding out a gold ax.

"No," answered the woodman, "that is not my ax. All the money I ever earned would not buy such an ax as that."

"I found another," said the man. "This must be the one," and he held out a silver ax.

"No, that is not mine," replied the woodman. "I am too poor a man to own such an ax as that."

"Well, here is another ax that I found. Is this yours?" The stranger held out an old ax of steel.

"That is mine, oh, that is mine!" cried the woodman, springing up joyously and taking his ax from the stranger. "Now we shall not starve. Thank you, kind sir. Where did you find it?"

The stranger said, "All three of the axes are yours. I am glad to make you a present of the gold ax and the silver ax. Let me have your hand. I am happy to meet an honest man."

The woodman's neighbors heard of his good fortune. One of them lost his ax. He appeared to feel very sad over his loss. He sat down by the roadside and bowed his head, looking out of the corners of his eyes for the stranger.

At last he saw the stranger coming around a bend in the road. The sun shown upon a gold ax which he carried in his hand. He stopped in front of the woodman. "Why do you grieve, my friend?" he asked.

"I have lost my ax with which I earned my living," the woodman replied.

"Cheer up," said the stranger. "I have an ax here. Is it yours?"

"That is the very one," said the woodman. "Thank you, stranger," and he reached out his hand to take the gold ax.

But the stranger drew back, and put the ax behind him. "It is not your ax. It is my own, and you wish to claim it. You are both dishonest and untruthful;" and he turned away.

THE FOX WITH HIS TAIL CUT OFF

Reynard lost his tail in a trap. Now a fox is proud of two things--his cunning and his tail. He had allowed himself to be trapped. This showed his lack of cunning, and he had lost his tail.

He was so ashamed of himself that he could not bear to meet another fox. He slunk off to his den and came out only when driven by hunger. When out hunting, he kept out of the way of all his neighbors. He did not mean that any of them should know of his bad luck.

At last he grew tired of living by himself. He wanted to gossip with his friends.

He wondered whether old Rufus was still running on top of the great meadow fence to throw the hounds off the track.

He longed to hear of the latest tricks of Fleetfoot's cubs. They were three of the brightest little foxes that ever lived. He wished that he could see them at their play.

He wished to know if the men were still cutting down trees near White-ear's den. If this went on, White-ear would have to find a new home. It would be hard for her after living in that beautiful spot so long.

If he were to hear the news at all, he must meet his comrades. "How can I bear to listen to their laugh!" he moaned.

He had not lost all of his cunning, as you will see. He lay for a long time with his head between his paws. His eyes were wide open, but he was not watching for game. He was thinking.

After a while he jumped up. He said to himself:

"I shall invite all of my friends to come to my home to-morrow evening. I shall tell them when they reach here that I can not get up to meet them for I have been very sick. They will all gather about me here. I shall sit upon my haunches so that no one will ever find out that my tail is missing. As they are to be my guests, I must be the spokesman. My friends have always thought me to be a very fine speaker. Many times my advice has been asked. I have given it, and it paid my friends to follow it. The thing which I shall advise to-morrow will surprise them, but I feel sure that I can get my friends to follow it. I will set to work now preparing for the feast."

Early the next evening Reynard gave a series of strange barks. This was an invitation to his home. The foxes came from every direction and met at the foot of an old oak.

Reynard's den was under this oak. He sat upon his haunches near the door to welcome his guests as they came, but he did not move.

"You all know, friends, why I do not rise to welcome you," he said. "I have been very sick, and if I move about it gives me a very bad headache."

Reynard asked his friends, who were standing around him, what they had been doing for the last week or so. They told many interesting stories of how they had escaped from traps and dogs and men.

A pile of chickens, turkeys, and ducks lay in sight not far away. As they talked, their eyes often wandered to these.

It grew late. The company became a little restless. At last Reynard said:

"Now, friends, before we take our evening meal, I have something to say for the good of all of us.

"I have been lying awake nights thinking what we could do to free ourselves from the weight of our heavy tails. Spring is here with its rainy weather. You all know how wet and muddy our tails become. Often I have had to give up a first-class meal and trot off home, hungry, to stay until my tail had dried. You have had to do the same. Many a poor fox has lost his life because of his long tail.

"Now, what do you say to having our tails cut off? Think what free lives we shall then lead. I will cut them off if you wish. The cutting will be almost painless, I am sure. Now let us have them off in a hurry before supper. After our feast, we shall have a great dance."

His visitors were silent for a moment. Some nodded their heads, showing that they were ready to part with their tails.

The oldest and wisest fox in the crowd had been looking at Reynard very closely. He was the only one of all that crowd to miss Reynard's tail. At last he spoke slowly:

"Your advice may be good, but before I reply, pray turn yourself around."

Poor Reynard saw that he was found out. He dared not refuse to do as he was told, so he turned about.

What a shout the foxes gave! Poor bobtail could not say a word. The foxes seized the turkeys, ducks, and chickens, and ran off home with their long tails behind them, and poor Reynard was never again seen by any of them.

THE BLACKBIRD AND THE DOVE

One day a blackbird and a dove called upon a peacock.
The peacock received both of them very kindly in his arbor.

"I have long wished to meet you," said the blackbird. "Many have told me of your beauty and of your grace. I find that they did not tell me half." He stroked the peacock's coat lovingly as he praised him.

The dove was silent.

At last they bade the peacock good-by, the blackbird making many low bows.

As they started home, the blackbird said, "I hope I may never meet that stupid peacock again. I can not bear him. Did you notice his feet? I felt like laughing every time I looked at them. His voice makes me shudder. What can anyone see to praise in that bird?"

"I did not notice his feet nor his voice," said the dove. "He has a noble form and his dress is very beautiful. The rainbow and the flowers are not more beautiful."

The blackbird turned away in shame. He wished to hear fault found with the peacock, but the dove gave only the highest praise.

THE GREEDY DOG

"What a good time I shall have eating this meat when I get home!" said a dog as it started to cross a stream of water.

He stopped suddenly and looked down into the water. There was his shadow. "That dog has a larger piece of meat than I," he said. "I want that piece of meat and I will have it!"

He growled, but the dog in the water did not move nor did he drop his piece of meat.

He snapped at the dog in the water. He was soon sorry for that, for the meat slipped from his mouth and sank to the bottom of the stream, and the dog in the water lost his meat at the same time.

THE GOOSE THAT LAID GOLD EGGS

One day a farmer bought a goose and took it home.

The next day the goose laid an egg of solid gold.

"That is a wonderful goose," said the farmer, and he took the egg to a jeweler to find out its value.

"It is pure gold," said the jeweler, and he paid the farmer a big price for it.

Each day the goose laid a gold egg. The farmer had a dozen.

"I shall soon be a rich man," he said, "but I do wish the goose would lay more than one egg a day."

After the goose had laid many eggs, the farmer said, "That goose has many more gold eggs for me. I will not wait for one a day. I will kill the goose, open it, and get all the eggs at once."

So he killed the goose and opened it, but what do you think? There was not one egg to be found.

THE DONKEY AND HIS MASTERS

"How I hate this early rising!" said a donkey, with a great yawn. "I wish I might sleep till sunrise. Here I am, harnessed and ready to start to town before the roosters crow. And why? To take a little fruit and a few vegetables to market. Isn't that a foolish reason for spoiling my dreams!"

The master was tired of his donkey, for he never seemed willing to do his work. "I do hate a donkey with his ears turned backward," he said. "He has no right to complain, for his work is really light, and he gets plenty of food and rest."

One day a tanner came along. He saw what a strong donkey the gardener drove, and asked his price. The gardener was glad to sell him. "I hope he will enjoy his new work," said the gardener. "He never seemed quite happy with me."

The tanner used the donkey to carry hides. These were heavy and bad-smelling. They almost made him sick.

"Oh, dear!" the donkey groaned one day. "I wish I were back with the gardener. The vegetables were fresh and I was often given a cabbage leaf or a beet top. I did have to get out early, to be sure, but I did not work late. Here I must work early and late, and if I turn out of the road to get a mouthful of grass, I am beaten soundly. I hate this work and this place."

The donkey was so ill-natured that the tanner sold him to a coal miner. He was lowered into a coal mine, where he had to pass his time pulling loads of coal. The mine was dark, and he was kept very busy.

"This is very bad," he cried. "I wish I were with the gardener, or even with the tanner. Anything would be better than working in this dismal hole in the ground." But there he ended his unhappy life.

THE COBBLER AND THE RICH MAN

A cobbler worked in his shop from morning until night, and as he worked he sang. Tired people who heard him were rested, and sad men and women were cheered as they came near the shop. Children visited him and watched him at his work and heard him sing. They called him "Jolly Gregory."

"How can he sing when he works so hard and makes so little?" many asked; but still his singing went on.

Across the road from the cobbler lived a rich man. His home was beautiful, his clothes fine, and his fare the best that money could buy; but never in his life had he been known to give to anyone who needed help. He was really poor, for he lacked one thing which he very much wanted--sleep. Sometimes he could not get to sleep until early morning; then his neighbor's song would waken him. He wished that sleep could be bought for money.

One day he said to himself, "I believe I will help that cobbler over the way. He has a hard time to make enough money to buy his food and clothes." So he sent for the cobbler.

"Honest Gregory," he said "how much do you earn in a year?"

"How much a year?" replied the cobbler, scratching his head. "I never reckon my money in that way. It goes as fast as it comes, but I am glad to be able to earn it. I cobble on from day to day and earn a living."

"Well then, Gregory, how much do you earn each day?" asked the rich man.

"Why, sometimes more and sometimes less," answered the cobbler. "On many days--the holidays--I earn nothing. I wish there were fewer of these; but then we manage to live."

"You are a happy man now," said the rich man, "but I will make you happier," and he handed the cobbler five hundred dollars. "Go spend this money carefully. It will supply your needs for many days," he said.

The cobbler had never dreamed of so much money before. He thought it was enough to keep him in food and clothes all his life.

He took the money home and hid it, but he hid his joy with it. He stopped singing and became sad. He could not sleep for fear of robbers. He thought that everyone who came into his shop was trying to find out his secret, or wished a gift. When a cat ran over the floor, he thought a thief had slipped through the door.

At last, poor man, he could bear it no longer. He took the money, hurried to the rich man, and cried, "Oh, give me back my songs and my sweet sleep! Here is your money, every cent of it. I made a poor trade."

The rich man looked at him and said, "I thought I had made you happy. I have not missed your songs, for, strange as it may seem, I have been sleeping soundly ever since I talked with you."

THE ICE KING

A tribe of Indians lived near a river. One winter the weather was very cold, and many of them died.

But spring came at last. The snow melted from the tops of the mountains and ran in torrents down their steep sides and into the river.

The ice in the swollen river broke up into large cakes which floated down the stream.

The weather grew warmer. All the ice melted except one big cake which the flood had left on the bank of the river.

The sun had been shining on this piece of ice for many days, but it would not melt. There were signs of spring everywhere except in this one spot.

A brave warrior had been watching this piece of ice. He said to himself, "That is the Ice King, I am sure. I must conquer him."

He raised his big war club and struck the Ice King, crying, "Come on, Ice King! Do your best. Freeze me if you can. I will show you that I am as strong as you are."

He struck again and again, and the Ice King began to shrink. Pieces of ice floated down the river. At last he became so small that the Indian picked him up and tossed him into the river.

"There!" cried the Indian, "off with you! Never dare to come back here again."

The Ice King whirled about and screamed, "I go now, but I shall come again. Look for me next winter. I will show you then which of us is the stronger."

The Indian hunted and fished all summer, but when autumn was near he began to think of the threat of the Ice King. "He will keep his word," said the Indian, "and I must get ready to fight him."

The Indian placed his wigwam among the trees, where it was well sheltered from the winds. Near it he heaped up a large pile of dry wood. Then he caught some large fish and tried out their fat so that he might have plenty of oil. He made thick clothes for himself out of the skins of animals. During the summer he had gathered much wild rice, and now he dried meat. While he was getting ready, the weather was becoming colder.

At last all was done, and the Indian said, as he sat by his blazing fire, "Let the Ice King come. I am ready for him."

That night the Ice King froze the little pools of water. After a few days the lakes and rivers were frozen. It was very cold.

One night when the Indian was sitting by his fire, the Ice King stepped to the door of the wigwam. He walked boldly to the fire and sat down opposite the Indian.

How cold the Ice King's breath felt! It nearly put out the fire. The poor Indian shivered, but he said to himself, "The Ice King shall not conquer me." He jumped up and threw dry wood on the fire. Then he poured oil upon the wood. The fire blazed up. The Indian put on more wood and more oil. The fire roared and crackled.

The Ice King began to feel too warm. He moved back a little way. The fire became hotter. The Ice King moved farther back. He began to sweat and to grow smaller and weaker. Then he cried out, "My friend, I am conquered. Let me go! Oh, let me go!"

The Indian arose and pushed the fire back from the Ice King. Then he took his trembling hand, lifted him up, and led him to the door of the wigwam.

As the Ice King passed out he said, "You have conquered me twice. You shall always be my master."

Ever since that time men have been masters of the Ice King. When his cold breath blows, they make the fires warmer and their clothing thicker.[2]

THE WOLF, THE GOAT, AND THE KID

"Good-by, little one," said Mrs. White Paw, the goat, to her daughter.

"Do not go, mother, I am afraid to stay here alone," cried little Nanny.

"But I must get my dinner or you will have no milk for your supper," said her mother.

"There is nothing to fear but the prowling wolf. Bar the door when I am gone; then he can not get in. Do not open the door unless you hear this password, 'Cursed be the wolf and all his race!'"

The mother, as she trotted away, felt no fear for her little daughter's safety. "No one knows that password but myself," she said; "but I shall be very glad when Nanny is old enough to go out with me to dine on the green hill. She is lonely when I am gone."

Little Nanny was not as safe as the mother thought, for slinking in the bushes near Mrs. White Paw's home was the hateful wolf. He heard the password which the mother gave to her little one, and laughed at the thought of the good feast which he should have by and by.

After the mother had been away for some time, the wolf sneaked to the door of the little house. He knocked, and gave the password, "Cursed be the wolf and all his race." in a voice much like that of Mrs. White Paw.

Nanny started to open the door, thinking that her mother had come home; but she stopped, for the voice had not sounded quite like her mother's voice. "I will make sure that it is no one but my mother," she said to herself. So she called, "Mother, show me your white paw before I open the door."

The wolf was angry, for he had no white paw to show. He gave a long, angry howl and went away.

The mother heard the howl as she turned her face homeward. "That will fright-

---

2 Adapted from "The Ice Man" in Legends of the MicMacs, published by S. T. Rand; permission to use given by Helen S. Webster, owner of copyright.

en Nanny," she said, and she hurried home. On reaching the house, she knocked and called in a cheery voice, "Cursed be the wolf and all his race."

Nanny did not open the door at once. She called back, "Show me your white paw, mother."

Mrs. White Paw put her paw to the crack in the door, and the door flew open.

"Why did you not let me in as soon as I gave the password, Nanny?" asked her mother.

Nanny told her of the wolf's visit. Mrs. White Paw was very proud of her wise daughter.

"Now have your supper, my brave Nanny, and go to bed. How glad I am that you are safe!" said the happy mother.

THE WISE GOAT

A goat was on top of a high cliff eating grass.

A wolf was at the foot of the cliff looking at him. He wanted the goat for his supper, but he could not climb the steep cliff.

"Come down here," said the wolf. "The grass is much better here. See how much of it there is."

"Thank you," said the goat. "You may have all of that good grass yourself, but you shall not eat me."

THE SHEPHERD AND THE DOGS

"Hero is a wonderful dog," said a shepherd, "I have not lost a sheep since I owned him, not one. Some foolish wolves tried to kill him when he was a puppy, but he treated them so badly that they have since been careful to keep out of his way."

"He is certainly a brave dog," said a neighbor, "but I think you are foolish to keep him. He eats as much meat as a dozen small dogs, and smaller dogs would take as good care of your sheep as he."

"There may be something in what you say," said the shepherd. "I have often wished that Hero ate less meat, but I should hate to part from him."

The next day the mayor of the town rode by. "What will you take for that dog of yours?" he asked.

"I can not spare him," said the shepherd; "he is too good a friend to part from. His only fault is a liking for meat."

"I will give you a hundred dollars for him," said the mayor, "and he shall have all the meat he cares to eat."

"You will not be foolish enough to refuse that offer, I hope," said the neighbor. "Think how much meat you will save."

"I think I shall have to let him go," replied the shepherd, slowly and sadly.

That night Hero was taken to the mayor's house and the shepherd received his money.

The shepherd found three curs in town to take Hero's place. He paid nothing for them, for their owners were very glad to get rid of them.

The next day the wolves said, "Hero is gone! Hero is gone! Now for a feast. We do not care for those cowardly dogs."

When the new dogs saw the wolves coming, they cried out, "Let us run," and away they all went.

When the sheep saw the wolves, they too began to run.

The shepherd was taking care of a lame lamb in a distant part of the field. When he saw the wolves chasing his sheep, he ran toward them; but before he could frighten the wolves away, they had killed several sheep.

"What a fool I have been," said the shepherd, "to let my neighbor do my thinking for me!"

THE BOY AND THE NUTS

A glass jar half full of nuts stood on a table.

Albert, who was very fond of nuts, saw it. He climbed up on the table and thrust his hand into the jar, grasping a whole handful. He tried to pull his hand out.

The mouth of the jar was too narrow for his fist.

He pulled and pulled and became very angry at the jar, but it was of no use.

At last he began to scream and cry. His mother hurried into the room to find out what was the matter with him.

"What hurts you, Albert?" she asked.

"This old jar will not let me have this handful of nuts," cried Albert.

His mother laughed when she saw the cause of all his trouble.

"Do you wish so many nuts?" she asked. "Try taking out a few at a time."

Albert did as his mother told him to do, and found that he could easily get the nuts.

"When you get into trouble again, my son, stop and think of a way out, instead of screaming," said his mother.

THE CROW AND THE PITCHER

No rain had fallen for many weeks. All the small streams and the ponds were dried up.

An old crow had been looking for water all the morning. At last he found some in a pitcher in a garden. He flew down to it and thrust in his bill; but he could not reach the water.

He walked around to the other side and tried again; but he could not get a drink. Oh, how very thirsty he was! It seemed as if he should faint.

"I must have that water. I will have it," he said.

Again he stretched his neck into the pitcher. No, he could not reach it.

He stopped a second and seemed to be thinking; then he said, "I will break the pitcher. My bill is strong and hard." So he gave the pitcher a hard thump. It did not break. He "thumped! thumped! thumped!" first here, then there. What a strong pitcher that was! It did not even crack.

"This will not do," he said. "I must try some other plan. I am big and strong. I will tip the pitcher over."

With that he pushed against it with his breast. It did not move. It seemed as if he must give up the attempt to get the water, but he did not once think of doing that.

Near by in the path lay some pebbles. The crow picked up one in his bill and let it fall into the pitcher. He dropped one after another into it. He could see the water rising a little. Now he worked harder than ever.

Before very long the water had risen so high that he could reach it with his bill. How refreshing it was! He drank as much as he wished, then flew away.

THE GROCER AND HIS DONKEY

A grocer went to a city not far away to get some salt. He took his donkey along to carry the load. On their way they had to cross a little stream over which there was only a narrow footbridge.

When they reached the city, the grocer placed some heavy sacks of salt upon the donkey's back and they started homeward.

On reaching the middle of the stream, the donkey stumbled and fell. As he arose, the water dripped down his sides and he noticed that his load had become much lighter.

The grocer had lost so much salt that it was necessary for him to return to the city and get a fresh supply. This time he put on a heavier load than at first.

When they reached the stream, the donkey said to himself, "This is a very heavy load that I am carrying, but I know how to make it lighter," and he lay down in the stream. When he arose, his load was much lighter, as he had expected.

"I will break him of that trick," said the grocer.

He drove the donkey to the city again, and heaped great bags of sponges upon his back.

The load was not very heavy, but the donkey said to himself, "I will make it still lighter."

When he came to the stream, he lay down again in the water. He started to rise, but to his surprise he could hardly get up.

"What can be the matter?" he thought.

His master, laughing, said, "Have you learned your lesson, old fellow? We shall see."

He drove the groaning donkey slowly back to the city, took the sponges from his back, and loaded him again with salt.

When the donkey came again to the stream, he picked his way carefully, for he did not wish to fall. This time he got across safely, and the grocer arrived at home with his entire load of salt.

THE THREE FISH

Three large fish lived very happily in a pond which few people ever passed.

One of these fish was always wise, the second was wise sometimes, but the third was never wise.

One day two men who were passing by the pond saw the fish.

One of them said, "Let us hurry home and get our nets. Those fish are too fine to lose." So they hurried away.

The three fish were very much frightened. The first one thought a moment, then swam through the outlet of the pond into the river.

When the men came back with their nets, there were only two fish to be seen. They found the outlet of the pond and made a dam across it.

The second fish now began to think; he came to the top of the water and floated on his back. One of the men picked him up in his net, but he seemed dead, so he threw him back into the water.

The fish that never thought sank to the bottom of the pond and was easily caught.[3]

THE WAGONER

"We must have coal," said the farmers to the wagoner.

"But the roads are very bad," replied the wagoner. "I never saw them worse."

"We can not wait for the roads to dry," said the farmers, "for without a fire we

---

3   Adapted from "The Three Fish" in The Tortoise and the Geese, published by Houghton, Mifflin Co

should take cold. Besides, we should have to eat uncooked food."

So the wagoner went into the country with a load of coal. He had not gone far when his wagon stuck fast in the mud.

"What am I to do now?" he asked himself. "I ought to have known better than to start out."

"Get up!" he cried to his horses. "Get up there, you lazy brutes! Pull out of here!"

The horses struggled hard, but they could not start the load.

"Hey there!" he called to a man who was working in a field near by. "Come and help us out of this mud-hole."

The man in the field had been watching the poor horses as they pulled with all their strength. He was angry at the wagoner for beating them so cruelly.

"Put your shoulder to the wheel," he called back. "When you have done all you can to help yourself, I shall be willing to help you."

The wagoner climbed down, muttering to himself, "I don't want to get down into this mud."

He put his shoulder to the wheel, pushed long and steadily while the horses pulled. Slowly the load began to move. Before long it was on firm ground.

The wagoner climbed up to his seat and called back to the man who was working in the field, "My load is out, but no thanks to you."

The man replied, "You took my advice and put your shoulder to the wheel; that is what brought you out."

THE LARK AND THE FARMER

A meadow lark built her nest in a field of wheat. She had a happy time raising her family, for no one came near her nest.

There were four little larks in her family, and they were now nearly large enough to fly.

The wheat was ripe and the mother knew that men might come to the field any day to reap; so she said to her little ones, "I am going out to get your breakfast. You must keep your ears and eyes wide open while I am gone; if you see or hear anything strange, you must tell me about it when I come back."

"All right, mother," said the young larks, "we shall do as you tell us."

The mother had been gone but a few minutes when the farmer who owned the field and his son came out to look at the wheat.

"This grain is ready to cut," said the farmer to his son. "This evening go to our neighbor, Mr. White, and ask him to cut it for us to-morrow."

The little larks were much frightened. They could hardly wait for their mother to get home.

"Oh, mother!" they called out as soon as they saw her; "do take us away from this field. The farmer has sent for Mr. White to cut this wheat to-morrow."

"If that is so," said the mother, "you need have no fear. If he waits for his neighbor to do his work, his wheat will not be cut."

Late the next afternoon while the mother lark was away, the farmer and his son came to the field again.

"Did you ask Mr. White to reap the grain?" said the farmer.

"Yes," replied his son, "and he promised to come."

"But he has not come," said the farmer, "and it is so late that I know he will not come to-day. The wheat will spoil if it is not cut. If our neighbors will not help us, we shall have to call upon our relatives. Go out this afternoon and ask your uncle John and his sons to cut the wheat for us to-morrow."

As soon as the mother came home, the little birds said, "The wheat will surely be cut tomorrow, for the farmer has sent for his relatives to cut it. Please take us away to-night, mother."

"Don't worry," said the mother; "there is no danger so long as the farmer waits for his relatives to do the work. We will stay right here to-night."

About noon the next day, the farmer and his son came to the field again. "This grain is still standing," said the father. "I told you to get your uncle John and his sons to cut it today. Why has nothing been done?"

"I called upon them and asked them to cut the wheat. They said that they would be here this morning. I do not know why they did not come."

"This grain must not stand another day," said the farmer. "It is shelling out now. You and I will come out here early to-morrow and cut it ourselves."

When the mother lark heard that the farmer had made up his mind to cut the wheat himself, she said to her little ones, "Get ready to fly away. If the farmer is to do the work himself, it will be done at once."

THE LION AND THE MOUSE

A lion was sleeping one day when a little mouse came along and ran up and down over his face.

This awakened the lion and made him very angry.

He put his paw over the mouse and said, "What do you mean by waking me? You shall pay for this," and he opened his big mouth to swallow the mouse.

"Oh, do not kill me, Mr. Lion!" squealed the mouse. "I did not mean to waken you. Do let me go and I will never trouble you again."

"No, I will not let you go," roared the lion.

"Please do," cried the frightened mouse. "If you will let me go perhaps I can do something for you sometime."

This made the lion laugh. "You do something for ME," he said. "What a joke! Well, you are such a little fellow that I will let you go this time, but never let me see you about here again," and he lifted his paw.

As the little mouse scampered off, he said, "Thank you, kind lion, I shall not forget your kindness."

Some time after this the lion was caught in a trap. The hunters tied him to a tree while they went to get a wagon to carry him away.

The lion roared so loud that the ground shook. The little mouse heard him.

"That lion is in trouble," he said. "I will see what I can do to help him," and he ran to the lion.

When the mouse saw that the lion was tied with ropes, he said, "Cheer up, Mr. Lion. Be quiet and I will set you free," and he began gnawing the ropes.

He worked long and hard and at last the lion was free.

THE ANT AND THE DOVE

An ant went to the river to get a drink. The water rushed along so fast that he was washed off the bank into the river.

"I shall drown!" he cried. "Help! help! help!" but his voice was so tiny that it could not be heard.

A dove was sitting in a tree that overhung the water. She saw the ant struggling, and quickly nipped off a leaf and let it fall into the water. The ant climbed upon it and floated down the river until the leaf was washed upon the bank of the stream.

The ant called out in its tiny voice, "Thank you, kind dove, you have saved my life;" but of course the dove could not hear him.

Several days after this, the dove was again sitting in a tree. A hunter crept carefully up to the tree. His gun was pointed at the dove and he was about to shoot, when he was bitten in the leg by an ant.

He cried out with pain and dropped his gun. This frightened the dove and she flew away.

"Thank you, kind ant," cooed the dove, and the ant heard and was glad.

THE HAPPY FAMILY

There was once a very queer family living in the woods. There were four in all--a rat, a raven, a tortoise, and a gazelle.

All day the animals were away from home hunting food.

The rat caught beetles which had hidden under leaves. He visited fields and barns Now and then he went to a henhouse.

The tortoise found plenty of insects in the woods and fields and did not object to a toadstool now and then.

The raven visited grain fields where he often met the rat.

The gazelle ate grass wherever he could find it. When he could not get grass, he ate the sprouts of trees.

At night all met at their home in the woods and talked of what had happened to them through the day. This is one of their adventures:

One day when the gazelle was out feeding, a hound scented his tracks and followed him. The gazelle heard the hound bark and darted off like the wind. The hound followed until worn out with running; then he gave up the chase. The gazelle stopped to eat grass. He was hungry and a long way from home.

That evening when the animals returned home they missed the gazelle.

The raven asked, "How does it happen that the gazelle is not home? Is he tired of us already?"

"No, indeed," said the rat. "I am sure that he is not. If I were a bird I should fly away at once to find him. I know that he would be here if he could get here."

"I will see if I can find him," said the raven, and he flew away. After a while he spied the gazelle, who had been caught in a net. He was trying hard to free himself, but the ropes that bound him were too strong for him to break. The raven flew back home to get the help of the rat.

"Oh, rat," he said, "follow me. Our friend, the gazelle, is caught in a net. Come and gnaw the ropes and set him free!"

The raven flew away and the rat followed. As the rat left home, he said, "Tortoise, you had better stay at home. You go so slowly that you can not reach the gazelle in time to help. We shall soon be back, I hope."

As soon as the raven and the rat were out of sight, the tortoise said, "I can not stay here and do nothing. I may be needed. I will hurry as fast as I can;" and he started off.

The raven reached the gazelle first. He said, "Cheer up, the rat is coming to set you free."

Soon the rat arrived. He began at once to gnaw the ropes. He had just set the gazelle free when a hunter came along. The gazelle sprang to one side into the bushes, the raven flew into a tree, and the rat ran into a hole in the ground.

The hunter looked about for the gazelle, but could not find him. He was very angry.

Just then the tortoise came up. The hunter picked him up and put him into his bag for his supper.

The raven whispered to the gazelle, "The hunter is carrying off our tortoise."

As soon as the gazelle heard this, he came out of his hiding place and limped along as if he were lame.

The hunter saw him. He threw down his bag and ran after the gazelle, thinking that he could easily catch him; but the gazelle kept ahead of him. At last the hunter could run no more. He went back to get his bag, tired and cross, but sure of a supper.

But what do you suppose had happened while he was gone? The rat had gnawed a hole in the hunter's bag and set the tortoise free, and both had run off.

It was now quite dark, and all the animals went home. That was the happiest evening of their lives. Each one had done something for the others, and all were safe, and it was good to be at home.

THE TYRANT WHO BECAME A JUST RULER

There was once a king who was so cruel to his people that he was called "The Tyrant."

The people used to wish that he would die so that they might have a better king.

One day he called his people together. They feared to go to him, yet they did not dare to stay away. When they were all standing before him, he arose and said:

"My dear people, I have been very unkind to you, but I hope after this to make your lives peaceful and happy."

The king kept his word. He sent good men to all parts of his kingdom to find out what the people most needed to make them happy. He then had everything done for them that a just king could do. He helped them to build good roads and bridges. He made their taxes lighter. He gave them a holiday now and then. The people learned to trust him and to love him.

One day one of his subjects said to him, "Please, O king, tell me why you are so much better to us now than you used to be."

The king replied:

"As I was going through a forest one afternoon I saw a hound chasing a fox. He caught the fox and bit him badly. The fox will always be lame.

"When the hound was going home, a man threw a stone at him and broke his leg.

"The man had not gone far when his horse threw him and his leg was broken.

"The horse started to run, but he stepped into a hole and broke his leg.

"I sat down by the road and thought about what I had seen. I said to myself, 'He who does wrong to any living thing will suffer for it sooner or later,' and that is why I am a better king and a happier man."[4]

THE HARE AND THE TORTOISE

"Why do you move along so slowly?" said a hare to a tortoise. "Let me show you how to get over the ground."

"You think I am slow, do you?" replied the tortoise. "Let us run a race to the cross-roads. I think I can beat you."

"Do you hear that?" said the hare to a fox, who was standing near. "Could any-one even think that such a slow-coach could beat me in a race?"

"It would be a good joke if he did," said the fox. "Do you wish to run a race? I will be the judge, if you care to have me."

"That suits me well," answered the hare.

"I am willing," said the tortoise.

So the fox marked off a place for starting, and set up a stake at the goal.

The hare and the tortoise stood side by side, and at the command, "Go!", from the fox, they began the race.

The hare bounded along and was very soon far ahead of the tortoise. He called back to the fox, "I think I shall take a little nap before I finish the race; the tortoise will not reach here for an hour or more." So he lay down in some bushes and went to sleep.

Every minute brought the tortoise a little nearer to the goal. He did not stop

---

4 Adapted from a fable of the same name found in The Tortoise and the Geese, published by Houghton, Mifflin Co.

for a second.

At last he passed the hare, but the hare still slept. On and on he plodded; it was a long way, but he had no thought of stopping.

He came nearer and nearer the goal. At last his foot touched the stake.

The hare wakened, stretched himself, and leaped toward the goal. "What, you here!" he cried when he saw the tortoise. "How did you ever reach here?"

"Just by keeping at it," said the tortoise.

THE MILLER, HIS SON, AND THEIR DONKEY

"I shall have to sell that donkey of ours," said a miller to his son. "I can not afford to keep him through the winter. I will take him to town this very morning to see if I can find a buyer. You may go with me." In a little while the miller, his son, and the donkey were on their way to town.

They had not gone far when they met some girls going to a party. They were talking and laughing as they went along. One of them said, "Look at that man and boy driving a donkey. One of them surely might ride."

The miller heard what they said, and quickly made his you mount the donkey, while he walked along at its side.

After a while they came to a group of old men who were talking very earnestly. "There," said one, "I was just saying that boys and girls have no respect for the aged. You see it is true in this case. See that boy riding while his old father has to walk."

"Get down, my son," said his father, "and I will ride." So they went on.

They next met some women coming from town. "Why!" they cried, "your poor little boy is nearly tired out. How can you ride and make him walk?" So the miller made his son ride on the donkey behind him.

They were now in town. A man coming down the street called to the miller, "Why do you make your donkey carry such a load? You can carry him better than he can carry you."

At this the miller and his son got off the donkey. They tied the donkey's legs together, turned him over on his back; and began to carry him.

A crowd soon gathered to see the strange sight. As they were crossing a bridge the donkey became frightened at the hooting of the crowd. He broke loose, fell into the river, and was drowned.

The miller was angry and ashamed. He said, "There! I have tried to please everybody and have only made a fool of myself. After this I shall do as I think best and let people say what they will."

THE PUG DOG AND HIS SHADOW

"I am going out to see the world," said a pug puppy.

He ran down a hill as fast as his wabbly legs could carry him, and looked into a little brook which flowed by.

"How queer!" he said, "I did not know that puppies live in water. This one looks just like my brothers, but it can not be one of them. They were all asleep when I came away. I will run home to tell mother about it," and up the hill he went as fast as he could carry his fat little body.

When he arrived at home, he panted out, "Oh, mother! I have found out something that you do not know. There is a pug puppy living in the creek."

"You are either dreaming, my son, or you have seen your own shadow," said his mother.

"I know what I saw, mother. I am not dreaming. It was not my shadow. It was a puppy dog," and the little pug barked savagely at his mother. "Come with me, mother. I will show you that I know what I am talking about." So the mother followed her puppy.

When they came near the foot of the hill, the little pug ran on ahead of his mother and looked into the stream.

"How lucky!" he said, "he is still here. Now, mother, you see that what I said is true."

"It is your shadow, little one."

"No, no, my eyes are better than yours, mother."

Just then his mother came up and stood beside him.

"How queer!" said the little dog. "That is the pug's mother. I did not see her before. It would be too cold for me down in that water. Why do they live there?"

"You foolish child," replied the mother. "It is our shadows that you see there. See, they are just like us."

"I am not a baby. I know what dogs are, mother. Those are real dogs."

"Watch, my son, and see what happens," and the mother dropped a stone on the two shadows. They were gone.

The little pug stood surprised. He dropped his ears and went slowly home without saying another word.

THE PARTRIDGE IN THE NET

"I have caught one at last," said a hunter, "and this is as fine a partridge as one often sees. It is a young one, too, I do believe," and he reached his hand into the net to take it out.

This frightened the partridge. It fluttered and cackled, pecking at the hunter's hand.

At last it cried out, "Let me go! Do let me go! I am but one little bird. If you will set me free, I will lead a large flock of partridges to your net, and will coax them to go into it."

But the hunter said, "You seem very willing to deceive the partridges; you might also deceive me. I will not let you go."

THE NORTH WIND AND THE SUN

"I am stronger than you," said the North Wind to the Sun.

"That is not true," said the Sun. "Everyone knows that I am the stronger."

"Show me that you are stronger than I," replied the North Wind. "You know very well that you are not."

"Do you see that traveler coming? I can make him take off his coat. You can not," said the Sun.

"We will see about that," answered the North Wind. "The one that makes the traveler take off his coat is the victor."

"All right," said the Sun, "and you may have the first trial."

"Whew! How the North Wind blows," said the traveler. "Whew! whew! Hold on there, North Wind; I would rather walk than fly. Whew! whew!

"How cold it is! I must button my coat uptight. Whew! whew! whew! I never felt such a wind before," said the traveler, as he folded his arms over his breast. "It seems determined to tear off my coat. I will turn my back to it. Whew! whew! whew! whew!" But the more the wind blew, the tighter the traveler held on to his coat.

At last the North Wind said, "I will try no longer, but you, Sun, can do no better."

The Sun said nothing, but came out from under a cloud and smiled down upon the traveler.

"How good that feels!" said the traveler. The Sun shone on. "It is getting warm," said the traveler, unbuttoning his coat.

It was now past noon. "The Sun is too much for me," said the traveler, and he threw off his coat and hunted for a shady place.

The North Wind's harshness had failed. The Sun's gentleness had won.

THE CAMEL AND HIS MASTER

One night a camel looked into the tent where his master was sleeping. "How warm it is in there!" he said. "I should like a good place like that myself."

The next night he put his head inside the door. "You will not mind my putting my head into the tent, I am sure," said he to his master. "The wind is cold tonight."

"Not at all," replied his master; "there is plenty of room."

In a little while the camel said, "Kind master, my neck is very cold; would you mind if I put it inside the tent?"

"Oh, no," said his master.

Now the camel seemed satisfied. But in a little while he wakened his master, saying, "My forelegs are getting cold. I should like to have them under cover."

His master moved over a little and said, "You may have a little more room. I know it is a cold night." So the camel moved a little farther into the tent.

Very soon the camel wakened his master again, saying, "I keep the tent door open by standing in the door. That makes it cold for both of us. Had I not better come wholly in?"

"Yes, come in," said the master. "There is hardly room for both of us, but I do not want you to suffer from the cold," So the camel crowded into the tent.

As soon as he was inside, he said: "Yes, I see there is not room for both of us inside the tent. If you were to go out, I should have a chance to lie down. So go!" And he pushed his master out of the tent.

The Codes Of Hammurabi And Moses
W. W. Davies

QTY

The discovery of the Hammurabi Code is one of the greatest achievements of archaeology, and is of paramount interest, not only to the student of the Bible, but also to all those interested in ancient history...

Religion   **ISBN: *1-59462-338-4***   **Pages:132**
MSRP $12.95

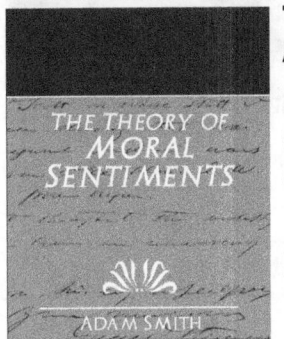

The Theory of Moral Sentiments
Adam Smith

QTY

This work from 1749. contains original theories of conscience amd moral judgment and it is the foundation for systemof morals.

Philosophy ISBN: *1-59462-777-0*   **Pages:536**
MSRP $19.95

Jessica's First Prayer
Hesba Stretton

QTY

In a screened and secluded corner of one of the many railway-bridges which span the streets of London there could be seen a few years ago, from five o'clock every morning until half past eight, a tidily set-out coffee-stall, consisting of a trestle and board, upon which stood two large tin cans, with a small fire of charcoal burning under each so as to keep the coffee boiling during the early hours of the morning when the work-people were thronging into the city on their way to their daily toil...

Childrens   ISBN: *1-59462-373-2*

Pages:84
MSRP $9.95

My Life and Work
Henry Ford

QTY

Henry Ford revolutionized the world with his implementation of mass production for the Model T automobile. Gain valuable business insight into his life and work with his own auto-biography... "We have only started on our development of our country we have not as yet, with all our talk of wonderful progress, done more than scratch the surface. The progress has been wonderful enough but..."

Biographies/   ISBN: *1-59462-198-5*

Pages:300
MSRP $21.95

The Art of Cross-Examination
Francis Wellman

QTY

I presume it is the experience of every author, after his first book is published upon an important subject, to be almost overwhelmed with a wealth of ideas and illustrations which could readily have been included in his book, and which to his own mind, at least, seem to make a second edition inevitable. Such certainly was the case with me; and when the first edition had reached its sixth impression in five months, I rejoiced to learn that it seemed to my publishers that the book had met with a sufficiently favorable reception to justify a second and considerably enlarged edition. ..

Pages:412

Reference   ISBN: *1-59462-647-2*   *MSRP $19.95*

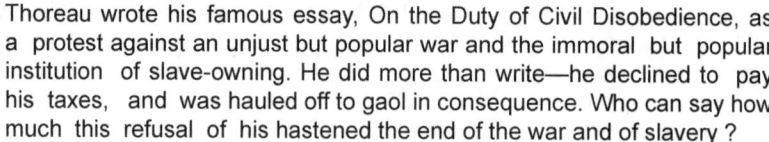

On the Duty of Civil Disobedience
Henry David Thoreau

QTY

Thoreau wrote his famous essay, On the Duty of Civil Disobedience, as a protest against an unjust but popular war and the immoral but popular institution of slave-owning. He did more than write—he declined to pay his taxes, and was hauled off to gaol in consequence. Who can say how much this refusal of his hastened the end of the war and of slavery ?

Law   ISBN: *1-59462-747-9*   **Pages:48**

MSRP $7.45

Dream Psychology Psychoanalysis for Beginners
Sigmund Freud

QTY

Sigmund Freud, born Sigismund Schlomo Freud (May 6, 1856 - September 23, 1939), was a Jewish-Austrian neurologist and psychiatrist who co-founded the psychoanalytic school of psychology. Freud is best known for his theories of the unconscious mind, especially involving the mechanism of repression; his redefinition of sexual desire as mobile and directed towards a wide variety of objects; and his therapeutic techniques, especially his understanding of transference in the therapeutic relationship and the presumed value of dreams as sources of insight into unconscious desires.

Pages:196

Psychology   ISBN: *1-59462-905-6*   *MSRP $15.45*

The Miracle of Right Thought
Orison Swett Marden

QTY

Believe with all of your heart that you will do what you were made to do. When the mind has once formed the habit of holding cheerful, happy, prosperous pictures, it will not be easy to form the opposite habit. It does not matter how improbable or how far away this realization may see, or how dark the prospects may be, if we visualize them as best we can, as vividly as possible, hold tenaciously to them and vigorously struggle to attain them, they will gradually become actualized, realized in the life. But a desire, a longing without endeavor, a yearning abandoned or held indifferently will vanish without realization.

Pages:360

Self Help   ISBN: *1-59462-644-8*   *MSRP $25.45*

QTY

The Rosicrucian Cosmo-Conception Mystic Christianity *by Max Heindel* ISBN: *1-59462-188-8* **$38.95**
The Rosicrucian Cosmo-conception is not dogmatic, neither does it appeal to any other authority than the reason of the student. It is: not controversial, but is: sent forth in the, hope that it may help to clear... New Age/Religion Pages 646

Abandonment To Divine Providence *by Jean-Pierre de Caussade* ISBN: *1-59462-228-0* **$25.95**
"The Rev. Jean Pierre de Caussade was one of the most remarkable spiritual writers of the Society of Jesus in France in the 18th Century. His death took place at Toulouse in 1751. His works have gone through many editions and have been republished... Inspirational/Religion Pages 400

Mental Chemistry *by Charles Haanel* ISBN: *1-59462-192-6* **$23.95**
Mental Chemistry allows the change of material conditions by combining and appropriately utilizing the power of the mind. Much like applied chemistry creates something new and unique out of careful combinations of chemicals the mastery of mental chemistry... New Age Pages 354

The Letters of Robert Browning and Elizabeth Barret Barrett 1845-1846 vol II ISBN: *1-59462-193-4* **$35.95**
by Robert Browning and Elizabeth Barrett Biographies Pages 596

Gleanings In Genesis (volume I) *by Arthur W. Pink* ISBN: *1-59462-130-6* **$27.45**
Appropriately has Genesis been termed "the seed plot of the Bible" for in it we have, in germ form, almost all of the great doctrines which are afterwards fully developed in the books of Scripture which follow... Religion/Inspirational Pages 420

The Master Key *by L. W. de Laurence* ISBN: *1-59462-001-6* **$30.95**
In no branch of human knowledge has there been a more lively increase of the spirit of research during the past few years than in the study of Psychology, Concentration and Mental Discipline. The requests for authentic lessons in Thought Control, Mental Discipline and... New Age/Business Pages 422

The Lesser Key Of Solomon Goetia *by L. W. de Laurence* ISBN: *1-59462-092-X* **$9.95**
This translation of the first book of the "Lemegton" which is now for the first time made accessible to students of Talismanic Magic was done, after careful collation and edition, from numerous Ancient Manuscripts in Hebrew, Latin, and French... New Age/Occult Pages 92

Rubaiyat Of Omar Khayyam *by Edward Fitzgerald* ISBN: *1-59462-332-5* **$13.95**
Edward Fitzgerald, whom the world has already learned, in spite of his own efforts to remain within the shadow of anonymity, to look upon as one of the rarest poets of the century, was born at Bredfield, in Suffolk, on the 31st of March, 1809. He was the third son of John Purcell... Music Pages 172

Ancient Law *by Henry Maine* ISBN: *1-59462-128-4* **$29.95**
The chief object of the following pages is to indicate some of the earliest ideas of mankind, as they are reflected in Ancient Law, and to point out the relation of those ideas to modern thought. Religiom/History Pages 452

Far-Away Stories *by William J. Locke* ISBN: *1-59462-129-2* **$19.45**
"Good wine needs no bush, but a collection of mixed vintages does. And this book is just such a collection. Some of the stories I do not want to remain buried for ever in the museum files of dead magazine-numbers an author's not unpardonable vanity..." Fiction Pages 272

Life of David Crockett *by David Crockett* ISBN: *1-59462-250-7* **$27.45**
"Colonel David Crockett was one of the most remarkable men of the times in which he lived. Born in humble life, but gifted with a strong will, an indomitable courage, and unremitting perseverance... Biographies/New Age Pages 424

Lip-Reading *by Edward Nitchie* ISBN: *1-59462-206-X* **$25.95**
Edward B. Nitchie, founder of the New York School for the Hard of Hearing, now the Nitchie School of Lip-Reading, Inc, wrote "LIP-READING Principles and Practice". The development and perfecting of this meritorious work on lip-reading was an undertaking... How-to Pages 400

A Handbook of Suggestive Therapeutics, Applied Hypnotism, Psychic Science ISBN: *1-59462-214-0* **$24.95**
by Henry Munro Health/New Age/Health/Self-help Pages 376

A Doll's House: and Two Other Plays *by Henrik Ibsen* ISBN: *1-59462-112-8* **$19.95**
Henrik Ibsen created this classic when in revolutionary 1848 Rome. Introducing some striking concepts in playwriting for the realist genre, this play has been studied the world over. Fiction/Classics/Plays 308

The Light of Asia *by sir Edwin Arnold* ISBN: *1-59462-204-3* **$13.95**
In this poetic masterpiece, Edwin Arnold describes the life and teachings of Buddha. The man who was to become known as Buddha to the world was born as Prince Gautama of India but he rejected the worldly riches and abandoned the reigns of power when... Religion/History/Biographies Pages 170

The Complete Works of Guy de Maupassant *by Guy de Maupassant* ISBN: *1-59462-157-8* **$16.95**
"For days and days, nights and nights, I had dreamed of that first kiss which was to consecrate our engagement, and I knew not on what spot I should put my lips..." Fiction/Classics Pages 240

The Art of Cross-Examination *by Francis L. Wellman* ISBN: *1-59462-309-0* **$26.95**
Written by a renowned trial lawyer, Wellman imparts his experience and uses case studies to explain how to use psychology to extract desired information through questioning. How-to/Science/Reference Pages 408

Answered or Unanswered? *by Louisa Vaughan* ISBN: *1-59462-248-5* **$10.95**
Miracles of Faith in China Religion Pages 112

The Edinburgh Lectures on Mental Science (1909) *by Thomas* ISBN: *1-59462-008-3* **$11.95**
This book contains the substance of a course of lectures recently given by the writer in the Queen Street Hail, Edinburgh. Its purpose is to indicate the Natural Principles governing the relation between Mental Action and Material Conditions... New Age/Psychology Pages 148

Ayesha *by H. Rider Haggard* ISBN: *1-59462-301-5* **$24.95**
Verily and indeed it is the unexpected that happens! Probably if there was one person upon the earth from whom the Editor of this, and of a certain previous history, did not expect to hear again... Classics Pages 380

Ayala's Angel *by Anthony Trollope* ISBN: *1-59462-352-X* **$29.95**
The two girls were both pretty, but Lucy who was twenty-one who supposed to be simple and comparatively unattractive, whereas Ayala was credited, as her Bombwhat romantic name might show, with poetic charm and a taste for romance. Ayala when her father died was nineteen... Fiction Pages 484

The American Commonwealth *by James Bryce* ISBN: *1-59462-286-0* **$34.45**
An interpretation of American democratic political theory. It examines political mechanics and society from the perspective of Scotsman James Bryce Politics Pages 572

Stories of the Pilgrims *by Margaret P. Pumphrey* ISBN: *1-59462-116-0* **$17.95**
This book explores pilgrims religious oppression in England as well as their escape to Holland and eventual crossing to America on the Mayflower, and their early days in New England... History Pages 268

QTY

The Fasting Cure *by Sinclair Upton*
In the Cosmopolitan Magazine for May, 1910, and in the Contemporary Review (London) for April, 1910, I published an article dealing with my experiences in fasting. I have written a great many magazine articles, but never one which attracted so much attention... New Age/Self Help/Health Pages 164
ISBN: *1-59462-222-1* **$13.95**

Hebrew Astrology *by Sepharial*
In these days of advanced thinking it is a matter of common observation that we have left many of the old landmarks behind and that we are now pressing forward to greater heights and to a wider horizon than that which represented the mind-content of our progenitors... Astrology Pages 144
ISBN: *1-59462-308-2* **$13.45**

Thought Vibration or The Law of Attraction in the Thought World
by William Walker Atkinson
Psychology/Religion Pages 144
ISBN: *1-59462-127-6* **$12.95**

Optimism *by Helen Keller*
Helen Keller was blind, deaf, and mute since 19 months old, yet famously learned how to overcome these handicaps, communicate with the world, and spread her lectures promoting optimism. An inspiring read for everyone... Biographies/Inspirational Pages 84
ISBN: *1-59462-108-X* **$15.95**

Sara Crewe *by Frances Burnett*
In the first place, Miss Minchin lived in London. Her home was a large, dull, tall one, in a large, dull square, where all the houses were alike, and all the sparrows were alike, and where all the door-knockers made the same heavy sound... Childrens/Classic Pages 88
ISBN: *1-59462-360-0* **$9.45**

The Autobiography of Benjamin Franklin *by Benjamin Franklin*
The Autobiography of Benjamin Franklin has probably been more extensively read than any other American historical work, and no other book of its kind has had such ups and downs of fortune. Franklin lived for many years in England, where he was agent... Biographies/History Pages 332
ISBN: *1-59462-135-7* **$24.95**

Name	
Email	
Telephone	
Address	
City, State ZIP	

☐ **Credit Card**   ☐ **Check / Money Order**

Credit Card Number	
Expiration Date	
Signature	

Please Mail to: Book Jungle
PO Box 2226
Champaign, IL 61825
or Fax to: 630-214-0564

ORDERING INFORMATION
web: *www.bookjungle.com*
email: *sales@bookjungle.com*
fax: *630-214-0564*
mail: *Book Jungle PO Box 2226 Champaign, IL 61825*
or PayPal *to sales@bookjungle.com*

Please contact us for bulk discounts

DIRECT-ORDER TERMS

**20% Discount if You Order
Two or More Books**
Free Domestic Shipping!
Accepted: Master Card, Visa,
Discover, American Express